Mister Pig

El señor Cerdo

TO THE
STARS

Written and Illustrated by
Teresa Weismann Knight

Edited by John K. Knight

Spanish Translation by
Camila Pilar Viola

Special Contributions by
Stacie Kelly

Dedication

This book is dedicated to my grandson
Forrest Darren Kelly

Preface

My husband John and I traveled to the Lesser Antilles, a group of islands in the Caribbean Sea. While he took French lessons on the island of Guadeloupe, I painted pictures and wrote stories.

A little girl about five years old named Maria was staying in a flat with her parents next to our *gite* (guesthouse). She spoke only French and I spoke English. We communicated through art and gestures. I drew pictures for her and she colored them. She called me, "Mademoiselle."

On the last day of our stay, I put our leftover food in a bag. Marie and I walked down the road to where there was a big pig and we gave him the leftover food. He grunted happily as he ate, while little piglets in a pen next to his watched and squealed.

As we drove away, I saw a couple of boys with bicycles throwing things at the big pig.

I wrote this story for Marie, but I never had an opportunity to show it to her. Maybe she will see it someday.

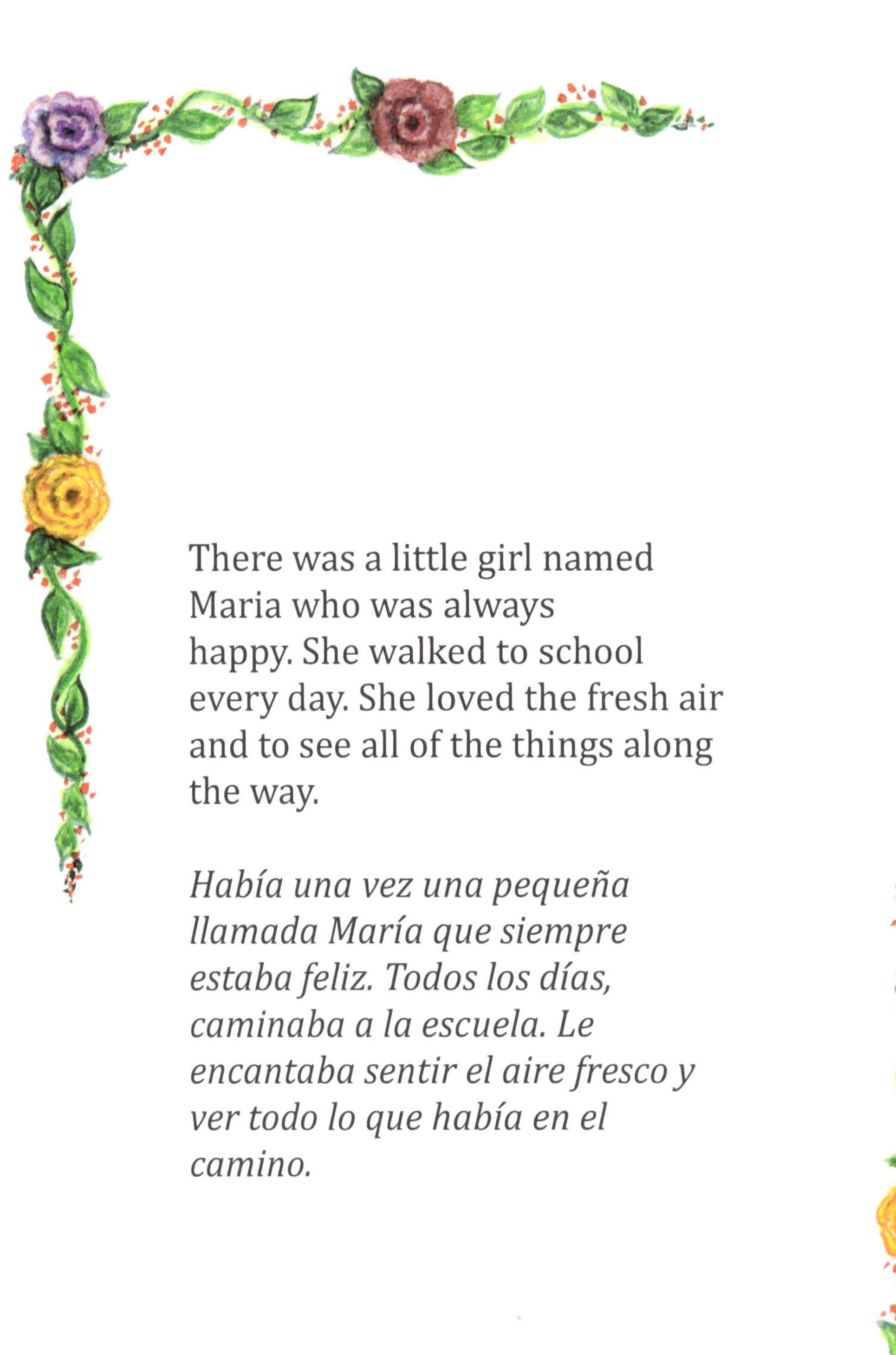

There was a little girl named
Maria who was always
happy. She walked to school
every day. She loved the fresh air
and to see all of the things along
the way.

*Había una vez una pequeña
llamada María que siempre
estaba feliz. Todos los días,
caminaba a la escuela. Le
encantaba sentir el aire fresco y
ver todo lo que había en el
camino.*

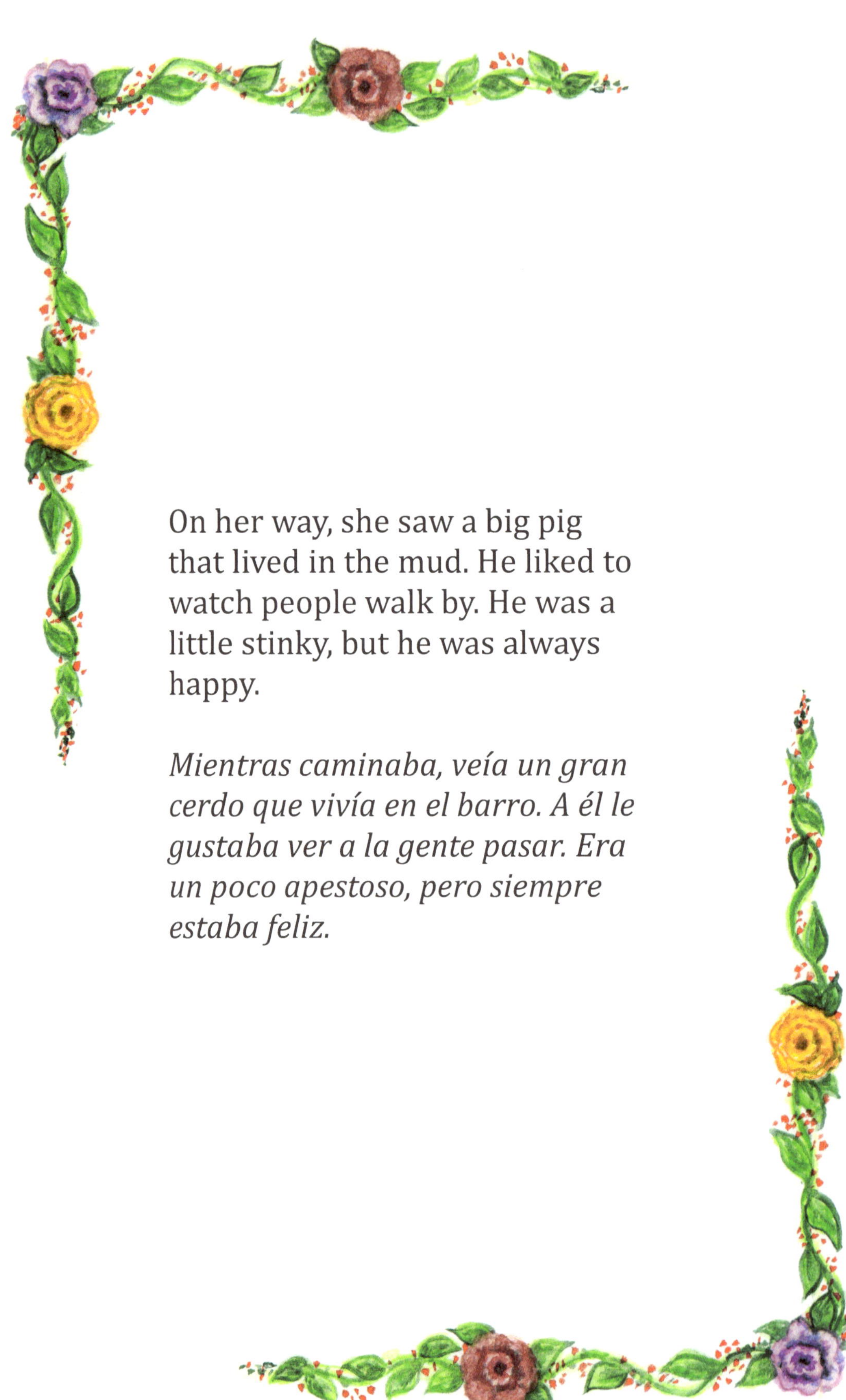

On her way, she saw a big pig
that lived in the mud. He liked to
watch people walk by. He was a
little stinky, but he was always
happy.

*Mientras caminaba, veía un gran
cerdo que vivía en el barro. A él le
gustaba ver a la gente pasar. Era
un poco apestoso, pero siempre
estaba feliz.*

 When Maria walked by the big
pig would grunt and say,
"Oink!" But she knew he was
saying, "Good morning!" And she
sang out, "Good morning, Mister
Pig!"

*Cuando María pasaba por su lado,
el gran cerdo gruñía y decía
"¡Oink!". Ella sabía que él le
estaba deseando un buen día.
—¡Buenos días, señor Cerdo!—
contestaba María.*

 A bunch of little piglets lived next to the big pig. They liked to squeal and see what was happening on the other side of the fence. The world looked so big out there!

Al lado del gran cerdo, vivían un montón de cerditos. A ellos les gustaba chillar y ver qué pasaba del otro lado de la cerca. ¡Desde allí el mundo se veía tan grande!

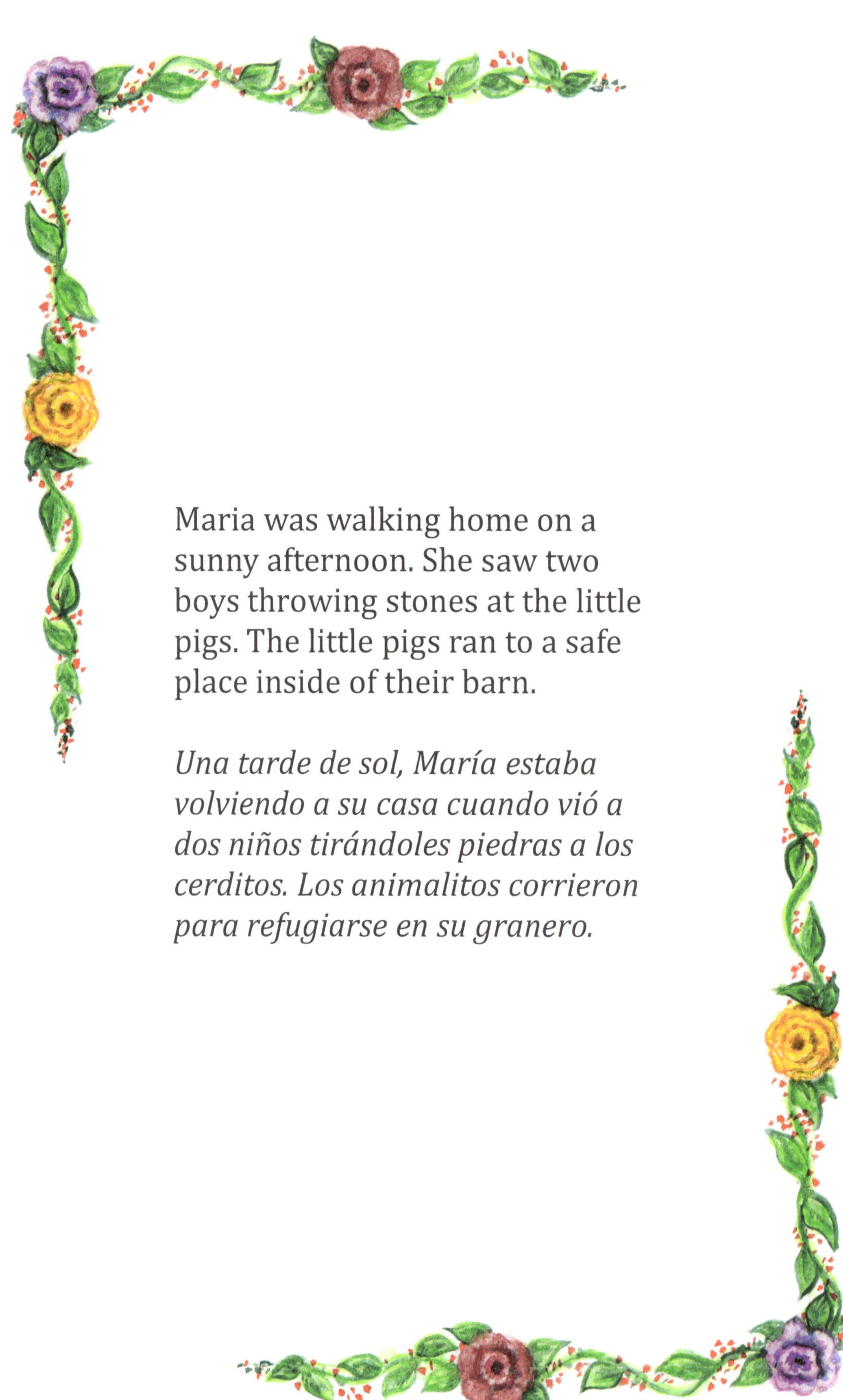

Maria was walking home on a
sunny afternoon. She saw two
boys throwing stones at the little
pigs. The little pigs ran to a safe
place inside of their barn.

*Una tarde de sol, María estaba
volviendo a su casa cuando vió a
dos niños tirándoles piedras a los
cerditos. Los animalitos corrieron
para refugiarse en su granero.*

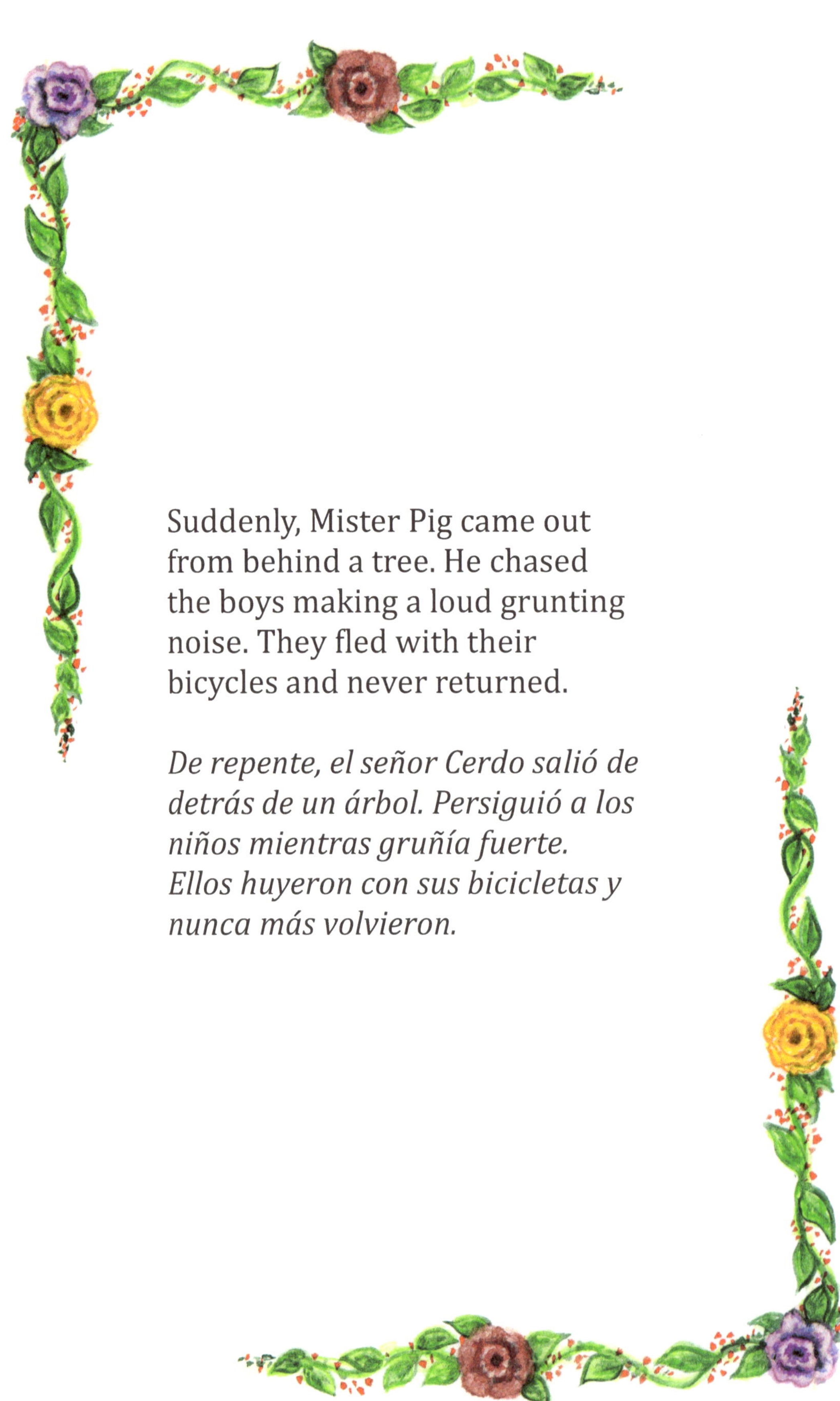

Suddenly, Mister Pig came out from behind a tree. He chased the boys making a loud grunting noise. They fled with their bicycles and never returned.

De repente, el señor Cerdo salió de detrás de un árbol. Persiguió a los niños mientras gruñía fuerte. Ellos huyeron con sus bicicletas y nunca más volvieron.

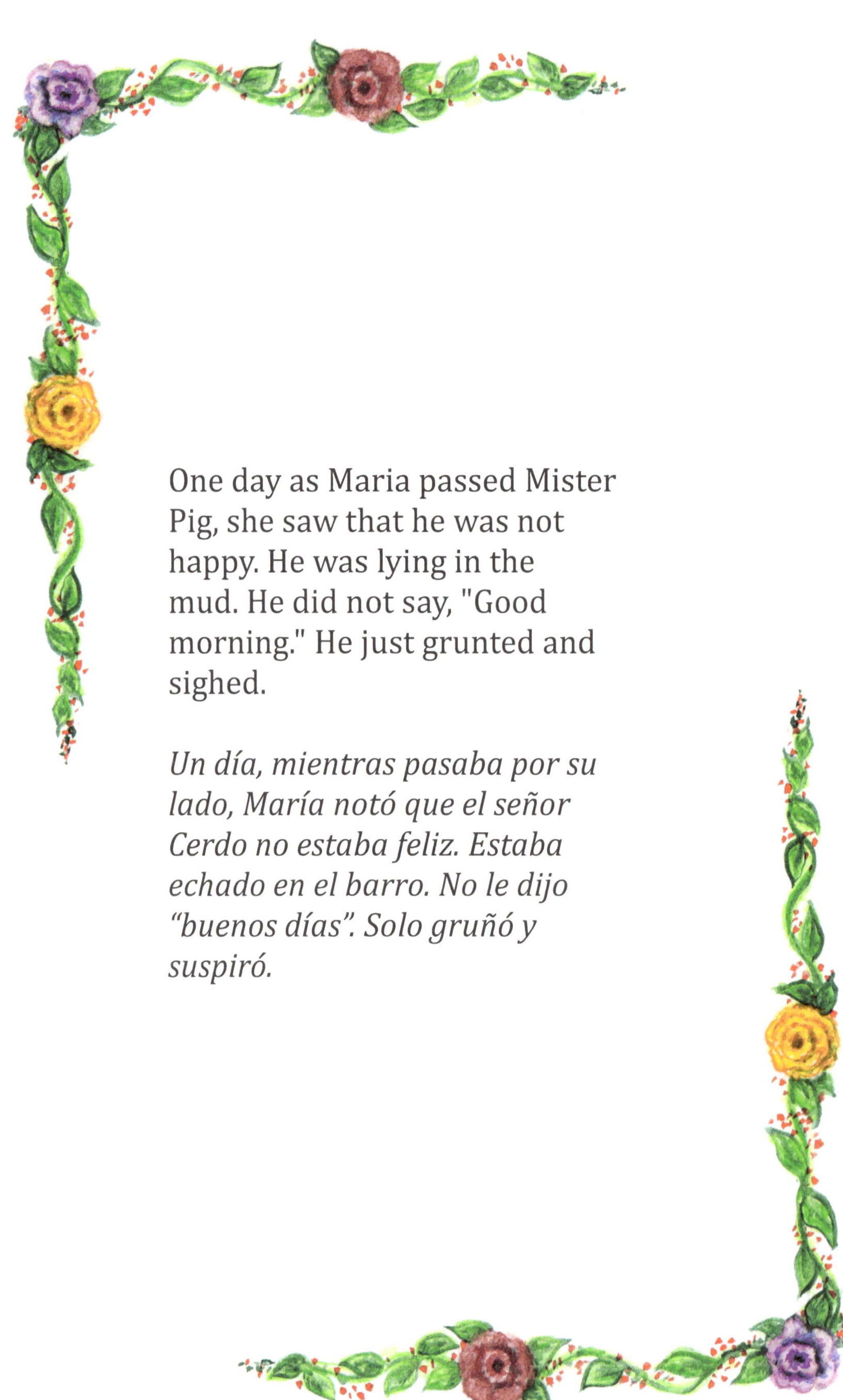

One day as Maria passed Mister
Pig, she saw that he was not
happy. He was lying in the
mud. He did not say, "Good
morning." He just grunted and
sighed.

*Un día, mientras pasaba por su
lado, María notó que el señor
Cerdo no estaba feliz. Estaba
echado en el barro. No le dijo
"buenos días". Solo gruñó y
suspiró.*

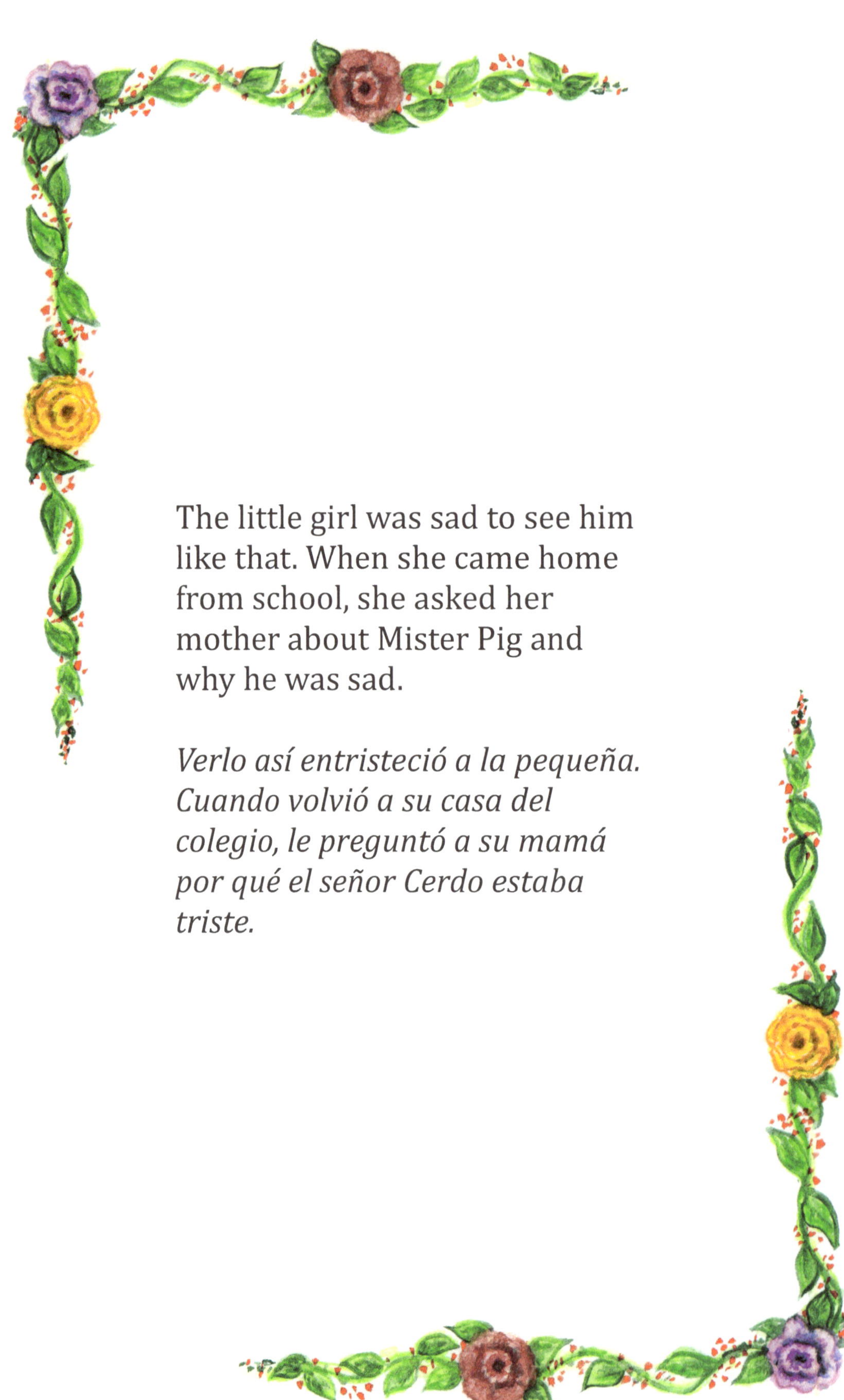

The little girl was sad to see him like that. When she came home from school, she asked her mother about Mister Pig and why he was sad.

Verlo así entristeció a la pequeña. Cuando volvió a su casa del colegio, le preguntó a su mamá por qué el señor Cerdo estaba triste.

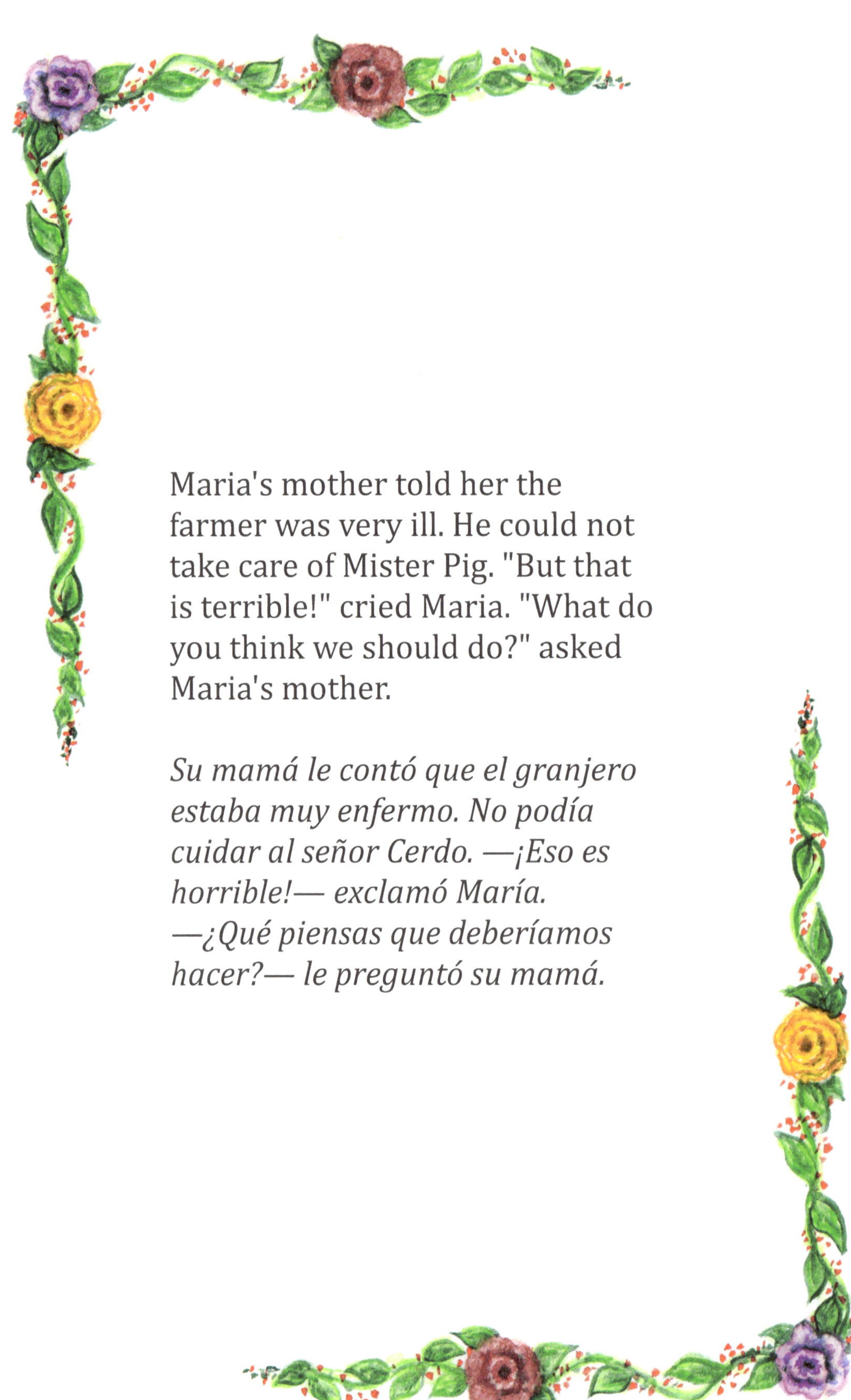

Maria's mother told her the farmer was very ill. He could not take care of Mister Pig. "But that is terrible!" cried Maria. "What do you think we should do?" asked Maria's mother.

Su mamá le contó que el granjero estaba muy enfermo. No podía cuidar al señor Cerdo. —¡Eso es horrible!— exclamó María. —¿Qué piensas que deberíamos hacer?— le preguntó su mamá.

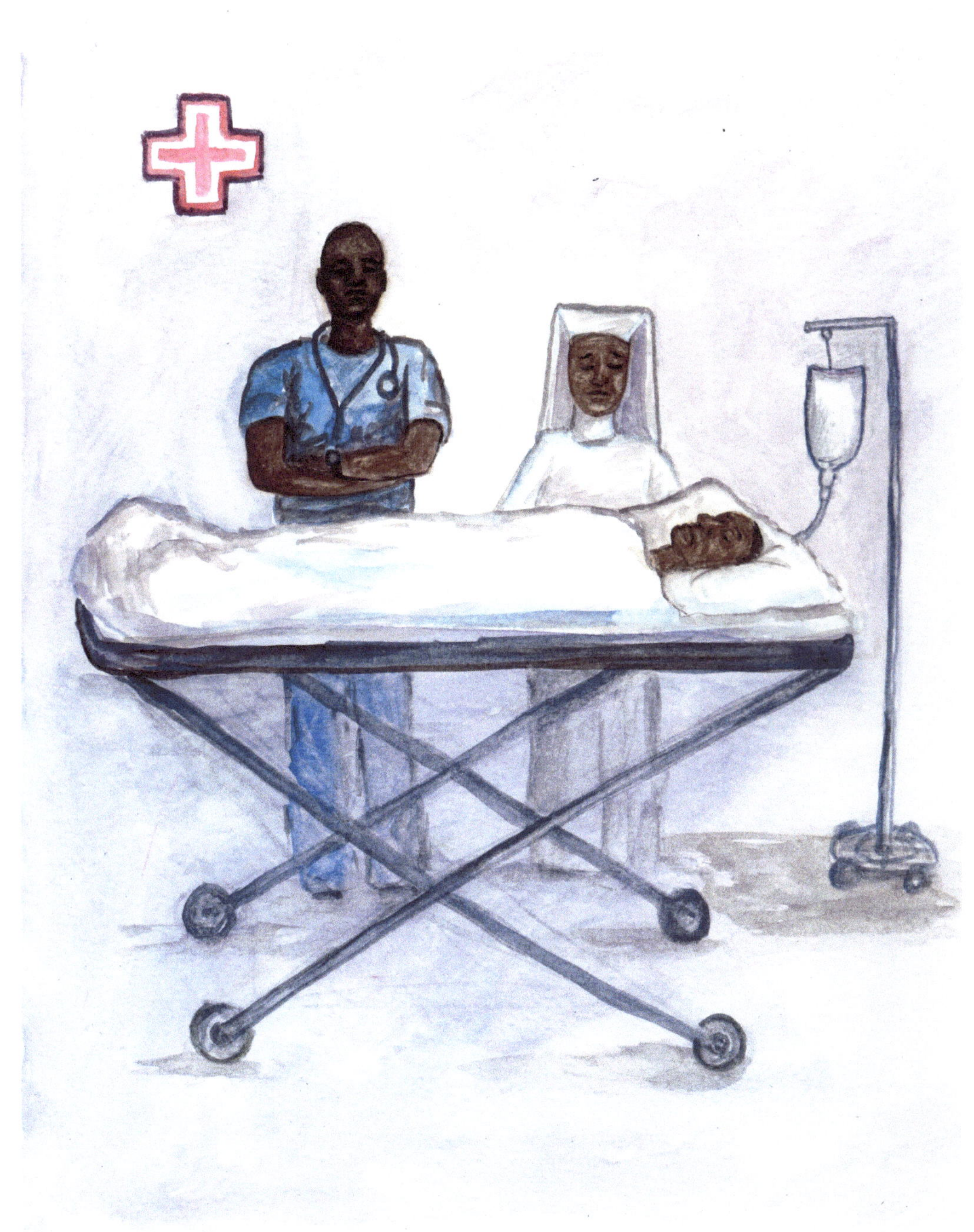

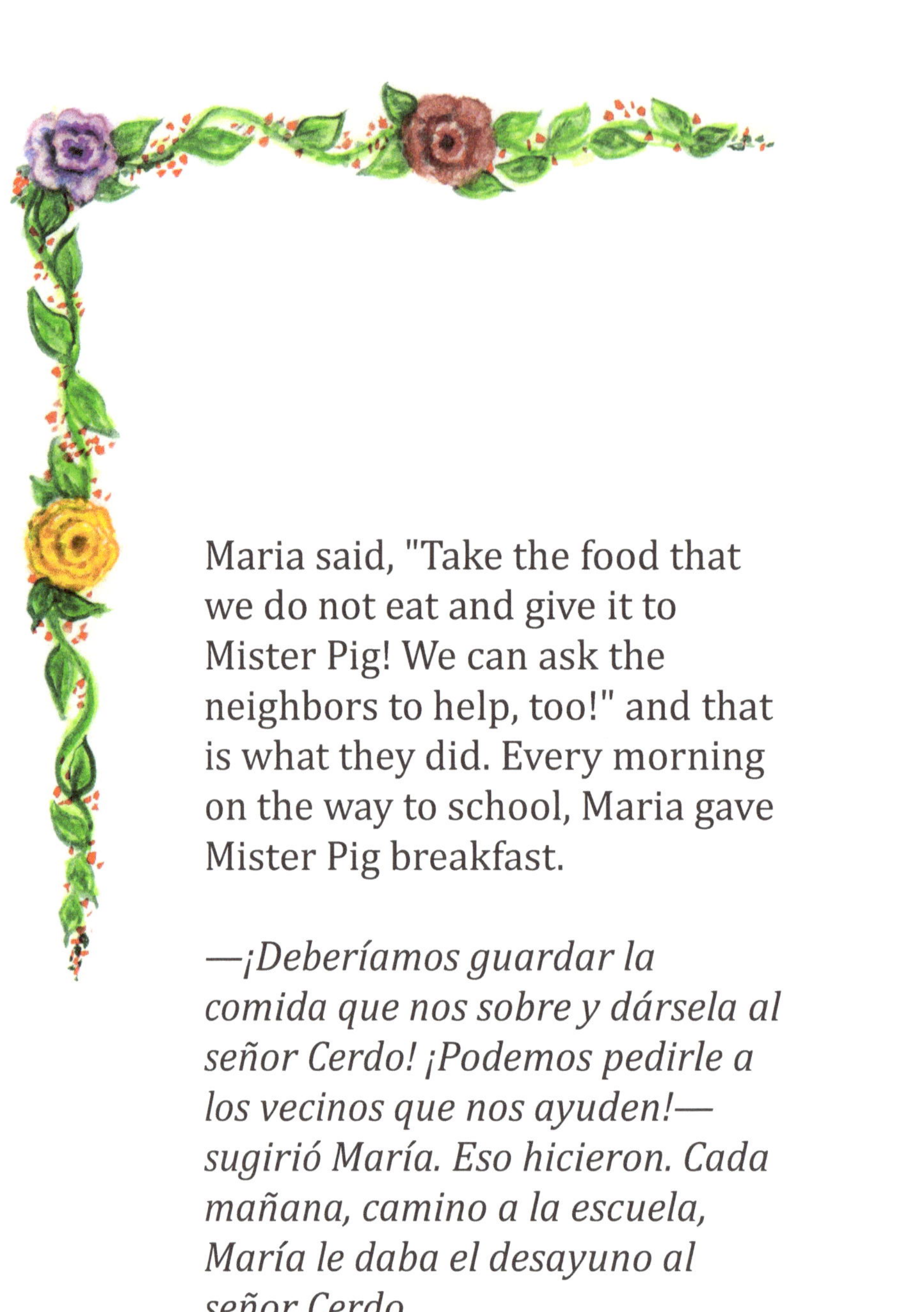

Maria said, "Take the food that we do not eat and give it to Mister Pig! We can ask the neighbors to help, too!" and that is what they did. Every morning on the way to school, Maria gave Mister Pig breakfast.

—¡Deberíamos guardar la comida que nos sobre y dársela al señor Cerdo! ¡Podemos pedirle a los vecinos que nos ayuden!— sugirió María. Eso hicieron. Cada mañana, camino a la escuela, María le daba el desayuno al señor Cerdo.

The neighbors gave him lunch
and dinner. When the farmer felt
better, he fed Mister Pig
again. Maria was happy she was
able to help the farmer and
Mister Pig.

*Los vecinos le daban almuerzo y
cena. Cuando el granjero mejoró,
volvió a alimentar al señor Cerdo.
María estaba muy feliz por haber
podido ayudarlos.*

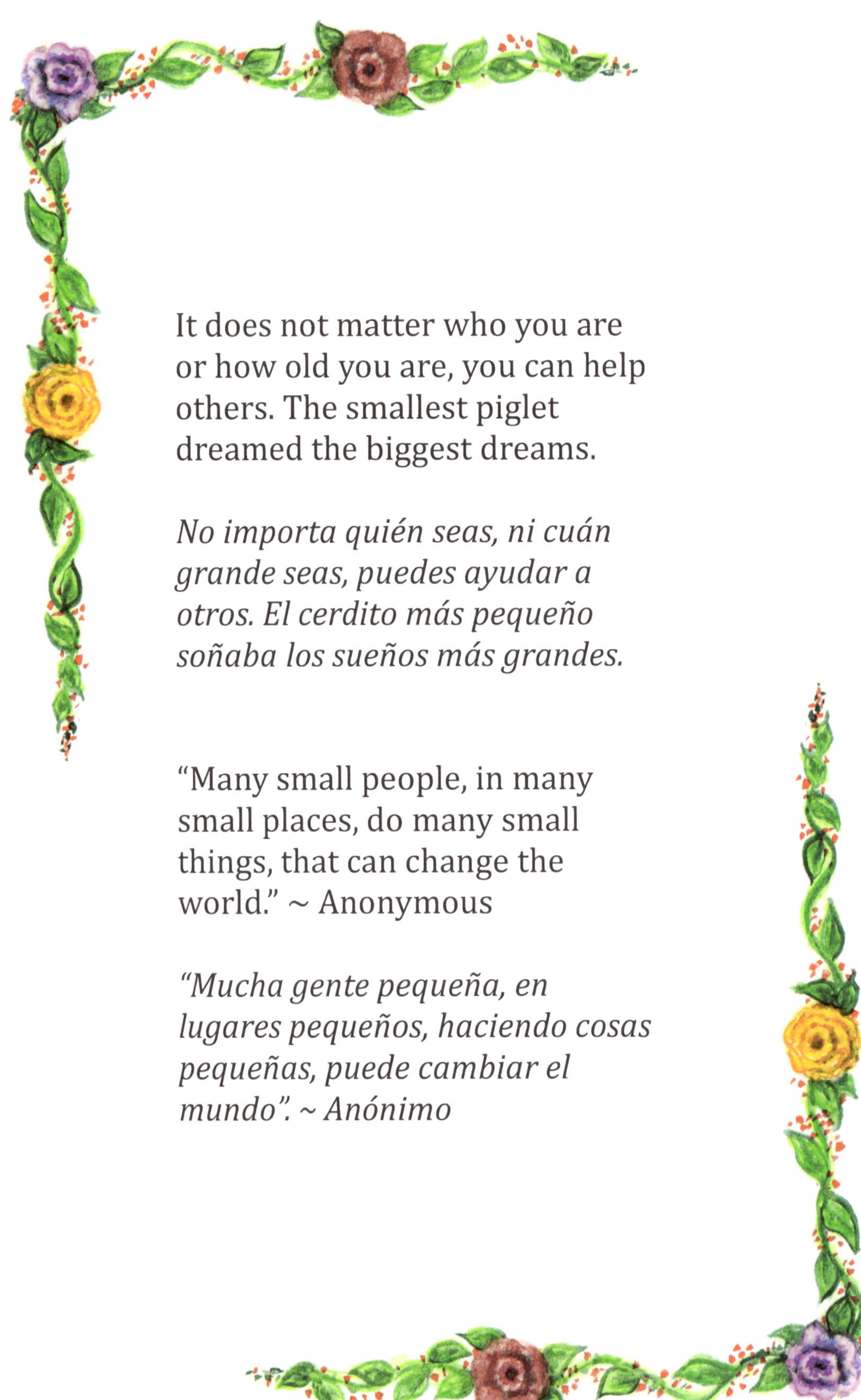

It does not matter who you are or how old you are, you can help others. The smallest piglet dreamed the biggest dreams.

No importa quién seas, ni cuán grande seas, puedes ayudar a otros. El cerdito más pequeño soñaba los sueños más grandes.

"Many small people, in many small places, do many small things, that can change the world." ~ Anonymous

"Mucha gente pequeña, en lugares pequeños, haciendo cosas pequeñas, puede cambiar el mundo". ~ Anónimo

The End

El fin

Other books published by Art & Photos, LLC available on Amazon.com:

Mr. Pig - *Monsieur Cochon*
Written and illustrated by Teresa Weismann Knight

Mars & Venus Circle Planet Earth
by Teresa Weismann Knight and John K. Knight

Asante Claws: A Swahili Christmas Story
Written and illustrated by Teresa Weismann Knight

Tails of Gus & Fanny: The Farmhouse
Patti Truedson Higgins, Author
Teresa Weismann Knight, Illustrator

Tails of Gus & Fanny: The Barn
Patti Truedson Higgins, Author
Teresa Weismann Knight, Illustrator

Raising Monarch Butterflies: A Personal Experience
Shirley Weismann, Author

Numbers Have Colors, Shapes & Textures
Written and illustrated by Teresa Weismann Knight

CarBON Art! Coloring Book
Written and illustrated by Teresa Weismann Knight

Starting Seeds Indoors Under Shop Lights: Easy - Low Cost
Shirley Weismann, Author
Sherri Thomas, Photographer